Tink's Treasured Friends

~ Book Twelve ~

DISNEY PRESS
New York

Illustrated by the Disney Storybook Artists
Designed by Deborah Boone

Copyright © 2010 Disney Enterprises, Inc.
All rights reserved. Published by Disney Press, an imprint of Disney Book Group.
No part of this book may be reproduced or transmitted in any form or by any means,
electronic or mechanical, including photocopying, recording, or by any information
storage and retrieval system, without written permission from the publisher.
For information address Disney Press, 114 Fifth Avenue, New York, New York 10011-5690.

Printed in China

First Edition
1 3 5 7 9 10 8 6 4 2

Library of Congress Catalog Card Number on file.

ISBN 978-1-4231-2320-0
F904-9088-1-10146

For more Disney Press fun,
visit www.disneybooks.com

Tinker Bell was on a mission. She was sailing in her homemade balloon in search of a lost treasure: an enchanted mirror that had one wish left to grant. Tink needed that wish! She had been put in charge of making the fall scepter for Pixie Hollow's Autumn Revelry. But just after completing it, Tink had accidentally crushed the scepter and shattered the one-of-a-kind moonstone that needed to be placed on top.

If only she could find the mirror and wish the moonstone back together! First, she needed to find the island north of Never Land where the mirror had been lost long ago. Luckily, she had the help of a stowaway firefly named Blaze, who was happy to shine his light on Tink's map.

Tink and Blaze flew on through darkness and fog that made it impossible to tell where they were. When the sun rose and the fog lifted, they discovered the balloon was stuck in a tree. But at least that meant they had reached land. Was this the lost island?

Tinker Bell anchored the balloon and flew off to look around. But while she was gone, the anchor came loose. Blaze tried to warn Tink, but it was too late: the balloon drifted away in the breeze, with Tink's compass, supplies, and pixie dust inside!

"We gotta find that balloon!" Tink said.

Tink and Blaze hadn't gone very far before a windblown leaf caused Tink to collide with a tree and fall into a faint. She dreamed of the argument she'd had with her friend Terence. Tink had blamed Terence for breaking the scepter, even though Terence really had been nothing but helpful to her.

Tink woke up feeling terrible about how she'd treated Terence and wishing he was with her now. On top of it, she was starving. Blaze offered to send out a call for supplies. Before she knew it, Tink was surrounded by friendly little bugs. They brought her some water and a snack. In no time, Tink was feeling refreshed and ready to continue her journey.

Tinker Bell remembered the story of the mirror that she'd heard back in Pixie Hollow. A rhyme that described how to find it had mentioned an "arch of stone." "By any chance, have you seen a stone arch around here?" Tink asked the bugs.

They had—and they began to lead her through the forest to find it. Tinker Bell had to walk since she had used up all her pixie dust. But at least she found a few things that had fallen from her balloon, including the compass. She removed the compass needle and carried it with her. It took longer to get places by walking than it did by flying. At last, Tink could see the stone arch! She was on the right track to finding the mirror!

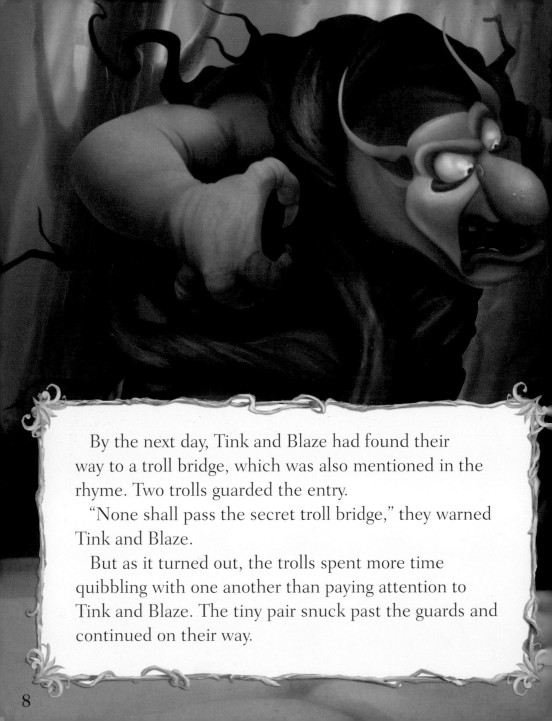

By the next day, Tink and Blaze had found their
way to a troll bridge, which was also mentioned in the
rhyme. Two trolls guarded the entry.

"None shall pass the secret troll bridge," they warned
Tink and Blaze.

But as it turned out, the trolls spent more time
quibbling with one another than paying attention to
Tink and Blaze. The tiny pair snuck past the guards and
continued on their way.

Then, after making their way through a dense thicket, Tink and Blaze came out onto a beach. There it was, just as the rhyme described—the pirate ship shipwrecked on the island with the magic mirror aboard!

At journey's end you shall walk the plank
Of the ship that sunk but never sank.
And in the hold, 'midst gems and gold,
A wish come true awaits, we're told.

"Okay, Blaze, this is it! We gotta find that mirror and fix the moonstone." It was Tink's last chance to complete her mission. She had to get back to Pixie Hollow with the repaired moonstone and fall scepter before the blue moon reached its peak! Otherwise, the blue moonlight wouldn't turn into the blue pixie dust needed to restore the Pixie Dust Tree!

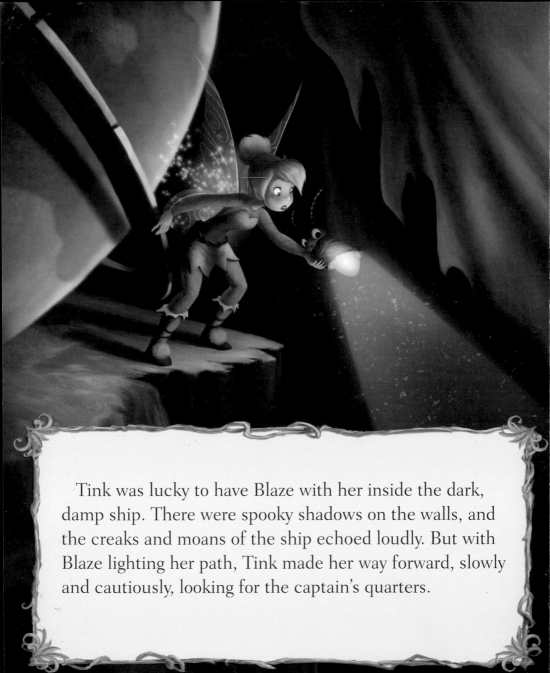

Tink was lucky to have Blaze with her inside the dark, damp ship. There were spooky shadows on the walls, and the creaks and moans of the ship echoed loudly. But with Blaze lighting her path, Tink made her way forward, slowly and cautiously, looking for the captain's quarters.

That's where Tink saw it: a satchel pinned to a table with a dagger. If it happened to be full of treasure, the mirror could be inside! The bag was just out of Tink's reach. Remembering the compass needle, she pulled it out, aimed, and threw it at the satchel. The satchel tore open and treasure spilled out!

There, among the gold and jewels and coins, was the mirror!

The mirror had only one wish left to grant. Tink pulled out the moonstone pieces and tried to concentrate on her wish. But all she could hear was Blaze's buzzing. Forgetting herself, she blurted, "Blaze, I wish you'd be quiet for one minute!" Magically, Blaze's buzzing suddenly ceased.

"That wasn't my wish!" Tink said with a gasp. But it was too late! Poor Tink! She had come so far—and now it felt as if it were for nothing. "I wish Terence were here," she cried. "I wish we were still friends."

As if by magic, Terence's face appeared in the mirror. "We *are* friends, Tink," he said.

But this wasn't magic. Terence was standing right behind Tinker Bell! But how?

Terence explained that he had found Tink's notes in her house and figured out where she'd gone. Then he had borrowed a little extra pixie dust from the Pixie Dust Tree to help him make the long journey to find her. He had even found Tink's balloon along the way!

There was no time to sit and chat. Taking the mirror, they made a quick exit, just escaping a pack of hungry rats. Terence led Tink and Blaze back to the balloon. With a sprinkling of his pixie dust, Tink's contraption was soon carrying them home to Pixie Hollow. Along the way, Tink worked out a plan for the fall scepter. With the mirror, the moonstone pieces, and help from Terence and Blaze, maybe there was a way to make it work.

Meanwhile, back in Pixie Hollow, the Autumn Revelry had already begun. The blue moon was almost at its peak! Just in time, Tink, Terence, and Blaze flew in on the balloon, making quite an entrance. Tinker Bell unveiled the fall scepter and everyone gasped. With the bits of moonstone and the frame from the magic mirror, plus Tink's original broken scepter which Terence had brought along, Tinker Bell had fashioned the most delicate and unusual scepter the fairies had ever seen.

Now the only question was: would Tink's scepter work— even though the moonstone was in pieces?

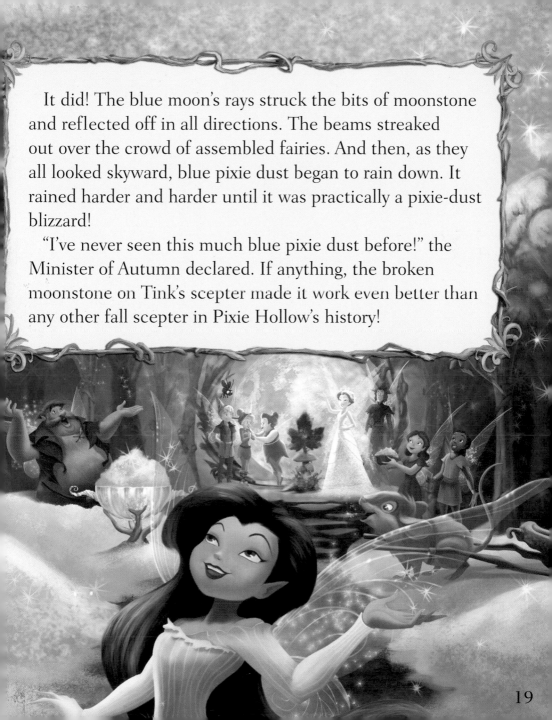

It did! The blue moon's rays struck the bits of moonstone and reflected off in all directions. The beams streaked out over the crowd of assembled fairies. And then, as they all looked skyward, blue pixie dust began to rain down. It rained harder and harder until it was practically a pixie-dust blizzard!

"I've never seen this much blue pixie dust before!" the Minister of Autumn declared. If anything, the broken moonstone on Tink's scepter made it work even better than any other fall scepter in Pixie Hollow's history!

And so, that night, the Pixie Dust Tree was restored. "Tonight, I believe, is our finest Revelry ever," said Queen Clarion, "thanks to one very special fairy, Tinker Bell."

But Tink made sure the queen mentioned her friends Terence and Blaze and their contributions to the night's success. Tink knew she couldn't have done it without them. And through all of her travels, trials, and tribulations, the greatest treasure Tink had discovered that day had not been the enchanted mirror, but the treasure of true friendship.